CASTLE GESUNDHEIT

Mark Fearing

CANDLEWICK PRESS

This is Castle Gesundheit, home of the Baron Von Sneeze.

And this is the home of Fiona and her family,
who live in the village of Handkerchief,
which is next to Castle Gesundheit.

The villagers in Handkerchief had put up with the Baron's snuffling, wheezing, and coughing day and night for as long as they could remember.

But no one ever dared to talk to the Baron about it — they were too afraid to visit the castle. So the villagers just did their best to ignore the constant noise.

After yet another night of not getting any sleep, Fiona had finally had enough . . .

The next morning, she marched to the castle.

But the drawbridge didn't lower.

AHH-AHHH-AHHHHHHHH-CHOOOOO!

Hello!?! Is anyone there?

Fiona tried to find a way in.

Nothing worked until . . .

she noticed a cat door

and squeezed through.

When she finally arrived inside, instead of finding crowds of knights, courtiers, and servants, Fiona found herself alone.

I am here to see the Baron. Hello?

Well, mostly alone.

Fiona followed the coughs,

nose blowing,

sniffles, and sneezing through the castle

until finally . . .

she found the source of all the noise.

VON SNEEZE

You must be the Baron Von Sneeze!

"I'm here to ask you to—"

"AHHH-"

"I wanted to talk about—"

"AHHHHHHH-"

"You have to stop your—"

"AHHHH-CHOOOOOO!"

"Sneezing! Stop your constant sneezing!" yelled Fiona. "You're keeping everyone in Handkerchief awake."

"Oh, I'm terribly sorry about that!" said the Baron. "I wish I could stop. I keep myself awake, too." The Baron sighed. "It's nice of you to visit, though. No one comes here anymore."

HONK!

As they walked through the castle, Fiona thought about how her mom and dad took care of her when she was sick.

"Do you eat chicken noodle soup?" she asked.
"Make it myself. Try some," said the Baron.
"It's very good," said Fiona.

"And do you use hot compresses and get plenty of rest?"
Fiona asked.

"Oh, yes, I'm always in bed by nine," said the Baron.

"Do you drink lots of water and keep your feet warm?"
"Yes," said the Baron. "I always wear wool socks.
Castles can be drafty, you know."

"Tell me all your symptoms," Fiona said. "My eyes are itchy and puffy. My nose is constantly running. And I sneeze all the . . . *aaaaachoo*—time!" Fiona thought for a moment. "Have you been to see the doctor?"

"I've tried all the best doctors and every cure imaginable.

I even consulted a wizard and a witch.

But nothing helped," said the Baron.

It seemed like the Baron had tried everything.
Fiona was out of ideas. Well, almost . . .
"You do have rather a lot of cats," Fiona said.

"Yes," said the Baron. "They have been our royal animal for a thousand years. And now they are my *o-O-CHOO*— only friends."

"I think I know what's wrong," Fiona said. "You're not sick. You're . . .

"But the Von Sneezes have always had cats!" the Baron protested. "They're on the castle banners, the royal seal, and the family crest!"

"I'm sorry, but I'm pretty sure they're what's causing your sneezing and itching," Fiona said.

"What can I do?" the Baron moaned. "I can't ask the cats to leave. Where would they go? Who would take care of them?"

"I have an idea . . ." said Fiona.

After the Baron said goodbye to each cat, which took a while, he didn't sneeze a single time once he left the castle.

It took Fiona's family only a
few minutes to pack up everything
they owned.

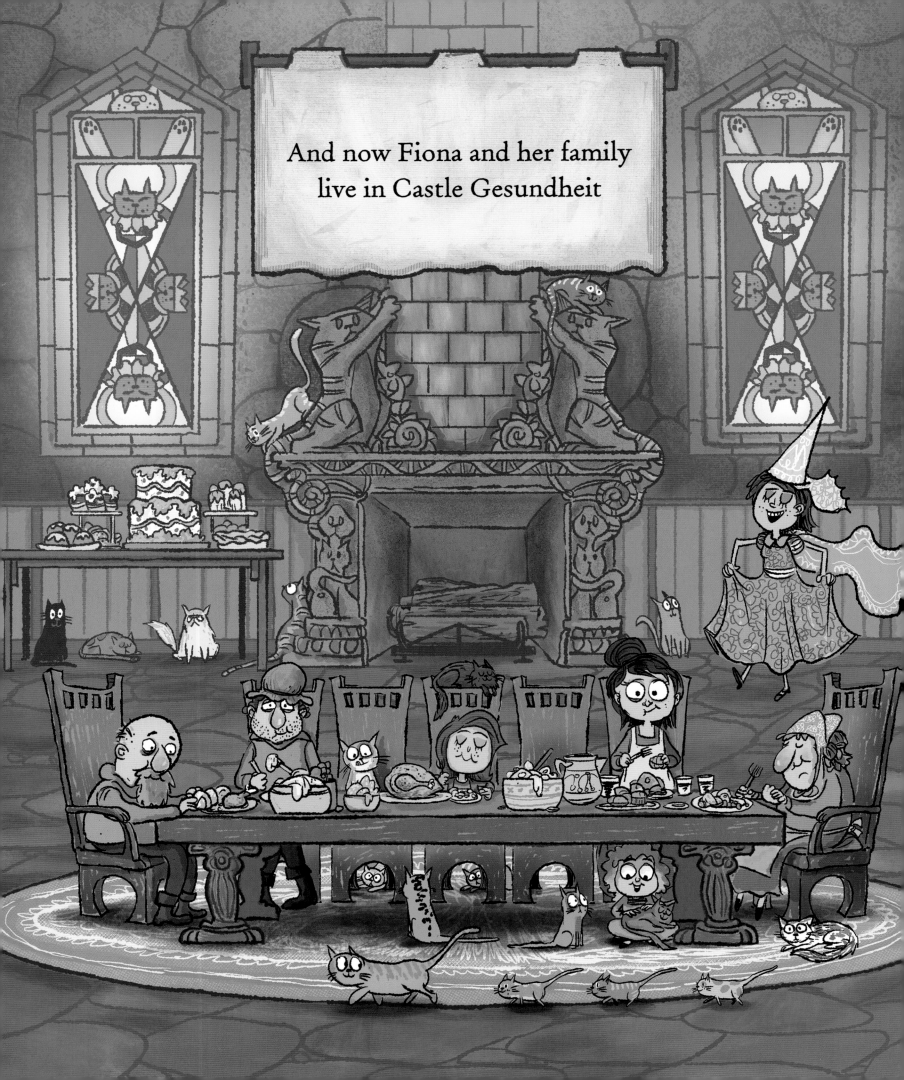

And now Fiona and her family
live in Castle Gesundheit

and the Baron lives in Fiona's old house.

And finally the village of Handkerchief is peaceful

and everyone gets enough sleep.

Well, almost everyone.

For Rowdy, Mabel, and Alexander
Not the cats we wanted but the cats we needed

Author's note:
A castle full of cats may seem fun, but please be sure to spay and neuter your pets!

Candlewick Press, 99 Dover Street, Somerville, Massachusetts 02144. www.candlewick.com.
Printed in Humen, Dongguan, China. 21 22 23 24 25 26 APS 10 9 8 7 6 5 4 3 2 1